FREE FALL

FOR KIM

Thanks to Matthew and Daniel

8 9 10 11 12 13 14 15

Library of Congress Cataloging-in-Publication Data

Wiesner, David. Free fall.

Summary: A young boy dreams of daring adventures in the company of imaginary creatures inspired by the things surrounding his bed.

[1.Dreams—Fiction. 2. Stories without words] I. Title.

PZ7.W6367Fr   1988   [E]   87-22834

ISBN 0-688-05583-4 ISBN 0-688-05884-2 (lib. bdg.) 0-688-10990-X (pbk.)

DAVID WIESNER

FREE FALL

LOTHROP, LEE & SHEPARD BOOKS   NEW YORK

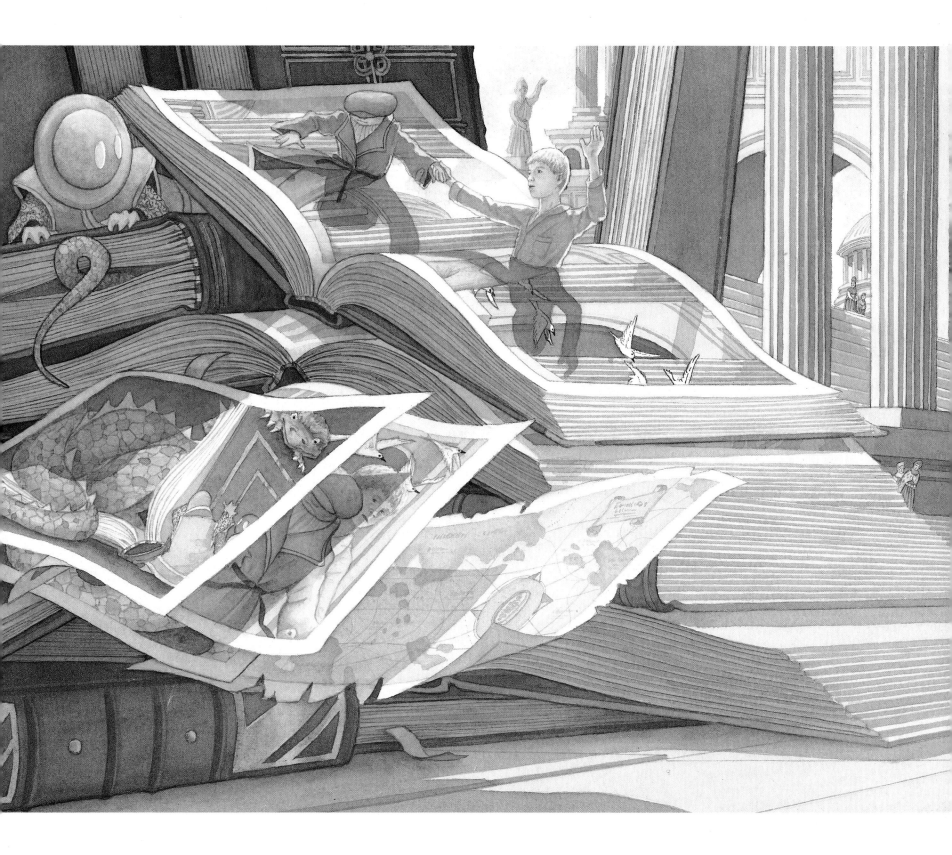